NATIONAL HOCKEY LEAGUE

By Kevin Frederickson

Kaleidoscope
Minneapolis, MN

Your Front Row Seat to the Games

This edition first published in 2020 by Kaleidoscope Publishing, Inc.

For information regarding permission, write to
Kaleidoscope Publishing, Inc.
6012 Blue Circle Drive
Minnetonka, MN 55343

Library of Congress Control Number
2019939028

ISBN
978-1-64519-073-8 (library bound)
978-1-64494-162-1 (paperback)
978-1-64519-174-2 (ebook)

Printed in the United States of America.

TABLE OF CONTENTS

CHAPTER 1

A Good Night For Hockey

The lights dim. Fans rise to their feet. The sound of skates scratching against the ice fills the arena. Then a roar from the crowd drowns it out. The Toronto Maple Leafs have taken the ice. They'll soon face off against the Pittsburgh Penguins. These are two of the best teams in the National Hockey League (NHL). Each team has big stars. **Veteran** Sidney Crosby leads the Penguins. Auston Matthews is a rising star for Toronto.

Finally, it's game time. The teams meet at center ice. A rush of energy fills the arena. The referee drops the puck. Game on!

FUN FACT

In 1973, the Chicago Black Hawks (now Blackhawks) became the first team to play the sound of a horn after a goal.

Sidney Crosby helped make the Pittsburgh Penguins an NHL power.

Crosby, left, and Maple Leafs defenseman Morgan Rielly battle for the puck.

The Maple Leafs take control. The home crowd cheers. Suddenly the Penguins have the puck. Some players step off the ice. Teammates climb over the boards and into the game. They chase the puck into the Maple Leafs' end.

Hockey moves at a rapid pace. The players go all out. They can only stay on the ice for short bursts. Then fresh teammates replace them. This keeps the game moving fast. One team races up the ice. Then the other races back the other way.

The players hit hard, too. A Pittsburgh player skates into the corner. He has nowhere to go. Suddenly a Toronto defenseman is charging. Bam! He **checks** the Penguins player into the wall. The glass shakes as their bodies hit. Fans stand up to cheer. But the game is already moving on.

HOCKEY RINK

Red Line
Goal Crease
Home Bench
Visitor Bench
Goal
Blue Line
Goal Line
Goal Line
Goal
Penalty Box
Blue Line
Goal Crease
Face-Off Circle
Face-Off Spot

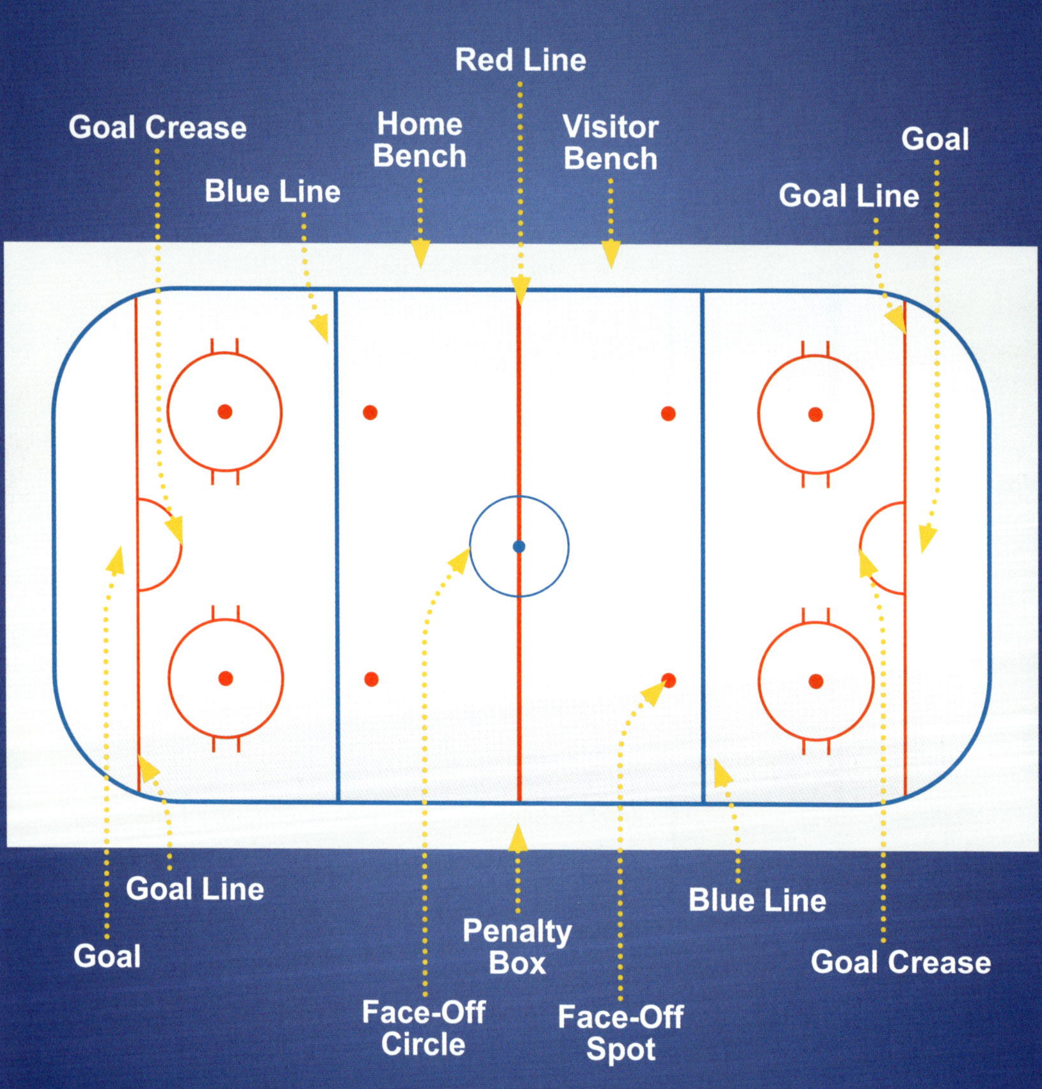

It's late in the first period. Toronto is trailing 2–0. But Matthews sees an opportunity. The young star skates toward the Penguins' net. He waits. Then a teammate fires a shot. The puck bounces off the goalie. Matthews is ready. He moves over to the puck. The goalie is out of position. Matthews slides the puck into the open net. Goal!

The goal sparked a comeback. Toronto scored two more goals. The Maple Leafs won 3–2. It was another thrilling NHL game.

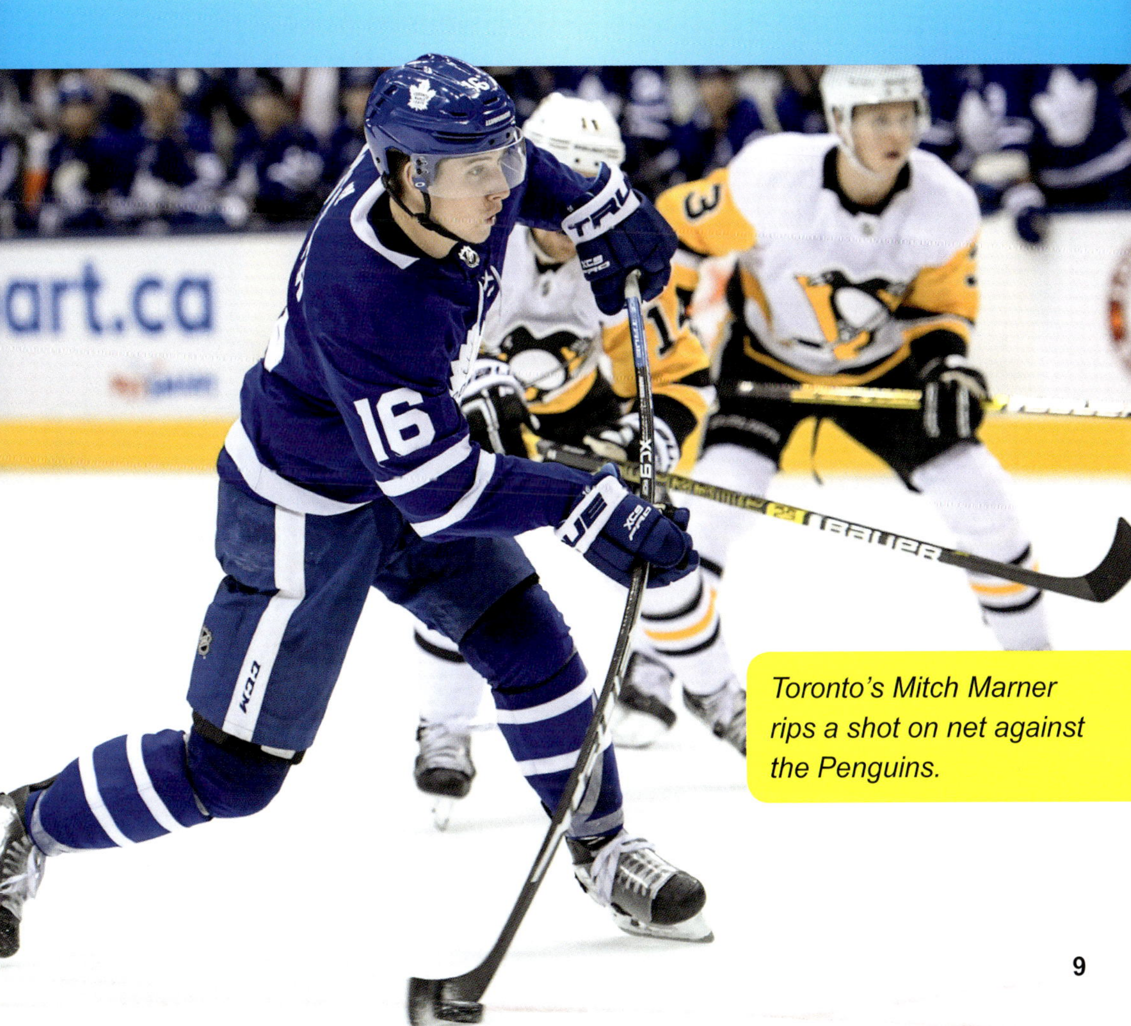

Toronto's Mitch Marner rips a shot on net against the Penguins.

CHAPTER 2

The Early Days

The puck landed just in front of the net. Gordie Howe acted quickly. The Detroit Red Wings winger flicked the puck. The Montreal Canadiens goalie had no chance. The puck flew into the top corner of the net.

Howe's goal was a big one. It was 1955. The Red Wings were in Game 7 of the Stanley Cup Final. Howe's goal gave them a 2–0 lead. Detroit went on to beat the Canadiens 3–1. That secured the Red Wings' seventh championship. Howe was key. His 20 playoff **points** set a new record.

Howe was an early NHL star. He joined the Red Wings in 1946. Together they won four Stanley Cups.

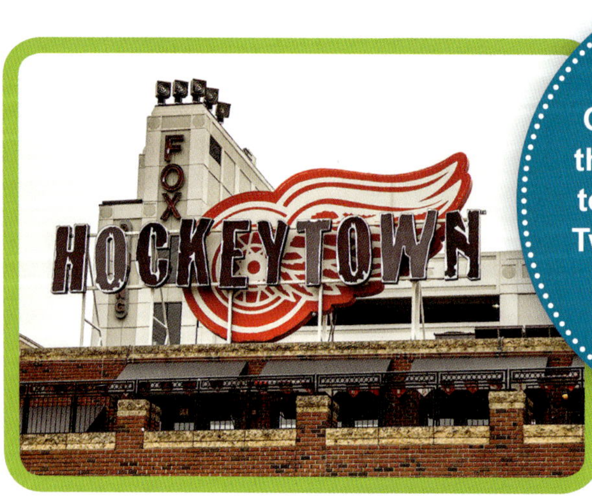

FUN FACT

Gordie Howe played thirty-two seasons of top-level pro hockey. Twenty-five were with the Red Wings. He retired in 1980 at age 52.

Gordie Howe led the NHL in scoring six times.

The NHL began in 1917. Teams struggled to make enough money. Some folded after just one year. In 1942–43, that changed. Six teams made up the league. It stayed that way for twenty-five seasons. Those teams became known as the Original Six.

The seasons got longer. Teams played 50 games in 1942–43. By 1949–50, they each played 70 games. That meant fourteen games against each opponent. Teams saw each other over and over. This led to fierce **rivalries**.

Brothers, from left, Reggie, Max, and Doug Bentley starred for the Chicago Black Hawks in 1942–43.

THE ORIGINAL SIX

TEAMS	FOUNDED	STANLEY CUP WINS*
Boston Bruins	1924	6
Chicago Black Hawks**	1926	6
Detroit Red Wings	1926	11
Montreal Canadiens	1909	23
New York Rangers	1926	4
Toronto Maple Leafs	1917	13

* From 1927 to 2019.

** The team changed its name to Blackhawks in 1986.

The Los Angeles Kings were among the NHL's six new teams in 1967–68. They joined the Minnesota North Stars, Oakland Seals, Philadelphia Flyers, Pittsburgh Penguins, and St. Louis Blues.

FUN FACT

The Original Six era ended in 1967–68. The NHL added six new teams that season.

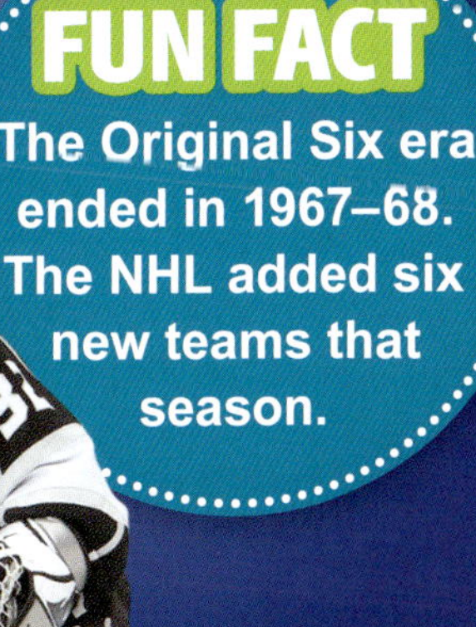

MADISON SQUARE GARDEN

HOME OF THE NEW YORK RANGERS

Built: 1968

The first New York City arena to carry this name opened in 1874. The Rangers first played at the third edition of the building on November 16, 1926. The current arena opened in 1968.

Renovation Cost: $1 billion

A three-year renovation was completed in 2013.

Capacity: 18,006

Madison Square Garden, or MSG for short, also hosts the New York Knicks basketball team.

Fun Fact:

Madison Square Garden is located above Penn Station, a busy train station.

Detroit and Montreal met on October 11, 1952. Fans at the Montreal Forum settled into their seats. So did fans across Canada. This game was special. It was the first to be broadcast on TV.

In 1959, the Canadiens were in New York. A Rangers player shot the puck. It hit Montreal goalie Jacques Plante in the face. Plante refused to keep playing. Finally, he gave in. He returned to the ice. But he did so wearing a mask. No goalie had worn one before. Now all goalies wear masks. Helmets took longer to catch on for the other players. They played with their hair flying free. Finally, in 1979, that changed. The NHL made all new players wear helmets.

THE STANLEY CUP

Hockey was a growing sport. But it wasn't very organized. Sir Frederick Arthur Stanley had an idea. In 1892, he bought a trophy. Today it is known as the Stanley Cup. Originally the best team from Canada won the trophy. That changed over the years. Since 1927, the NHL champ wins the Cup. It is a special honor. Everyone on the team gets to add their name.

CHAPTER 3

Maurice "Rocket" Richard won eight Stanley Cups in eighteen seasons with the Canadiens.

Success in Many Places

Jean Beliveau passed the puck. Montreal teammate Bernie "Boom Boom" Geoffrion got it. But a hard check knocked him away. No problem. Maurice "Rocket" Richard was right there. He shot the puck into the net. Goal!

That put Montreal up 2–0 on the Detroit Red Wings. The team would go on to win 3–1. That gave the Canadiens the 1956 Stanley Cup. And they were just getting started. Montreal won the next four Stanley Cups, too. No NHL team had ever done that.

Fans in Montreal got used to the winning. In 1993, the team won another Cup. It was their twenty-fourth. No other team comes close.

FUN FACT

In 1944–45, Maurice "Rocket" Richard became the first player to score fifty goals in fifty games.

Montreal has featured several **dynasties**. Other teams have had great runs, too. Mike Bossy was never the biggest player. But few could skate like he did. And he had a lightning-quick shot. Bossy starred for the New York Islanders. They won the 1980 Stanley Cup. Then they won the next three. Not even Wayne Gretzky could match that.

Gretzky was hockey's greatest scorer. He led the league in points at age nineteen. And he was just getting started.

The center went on to do it again ten more times. In 1983, he was still a young player. His Edmonton Oilers reached their first Stanley Cup Final. Bossy and the Islanders swept them in four games.

Gretzky learned from that experience. The Oilers won four of the next five Stanley Cups. They also won again in 1990. However, Gretzky was gone by then.

Mike Bossy (22) slides the puck past a New Jersey Devils goalie.

Patrick Kane glides into the offensive zone. He zips a shot toward the goal. Nobody can see where it went. But Kane does. He raises his arms. The Chicago Blackhawks have just won the 2010 Stanley Cup! This was just the beginning. Chicago won two more in the next five seasons.

Dynasties are harder to build today. The league has a **salary cap**. Players switch teams more frequently, too.

Chicago became a modern dynasty. Other teams have had success, too. The Detroit Red Wings made the 1991 playoffs. Then they qualified in 1992. In fact, they went back to the postseason every year through 2016. Detroit won four Stanley Cups in that time.

FUN FACT

Wayne Gretzky set an NHL record with 894 goals during his twenty-year career.

Jonathan Toews, left, and Patrick Kane were the centerpieces for the Chicago Blackhawks' three Stanley Cup wins.

CHAPTER 4

Growing the Game

Ryan Miller adjusts his mask. Then he adjusts his stocking cap. The Buffalo Sabres goalie is ready to go. So are more than 71,000 fans. This isn't just a typical game. A light snow falls on Miller. His team is outside. The rink is set up in a giant football stadium. The Sabres are about to host the first Winter Classic.

Many kids learn to skate outdoors. But NHL games are held inside. That changed in 2003. The Edmonton Oilers hosted an outdoor game. It was a huge success. The league decided to do more.

In 2008, the Winter Classic was born. Other outdoor games followed. They often take place in football or baseball stadiums.

FUN FACT
The Winter Classic is traditionally played on New Year's Day.

Ryan Miller makes a glove save during the 2008 Winter Classic.

There is no snow on Las Vegas Boulevard. And the only ice is inside T-Mobile Arena. Las Vegas has long been a popular vacation spot. Since 2017, hockey fans have been flocking there, too. That's when the Vegas Golden Knights **debuted**. They became the city's first major pro team.

Hockey is a cold-weather game. Until 1967, the NHL was only in cold-weather cities. Not anymore. Las Vegas is only the latest hot city to get an NHL team. The Los Angeles Kings were first. They started in 1967. Things really heated up in the 1990s. Warm states such as Arizona, Florida, and Texas got teams. These teams have helped hockey grow.

There is no ice to be found outside the Vegas Golden Knights' new arena.

HOCKEY FOR EVERYONE

Women play hockey, too. They haven't had the same opportunities as men. Men's hockey became an Olympic sport in 1920. Women had to wait until 1998. Some women's pro leagues followed. However, people are still working to ensure women have a stable league to play in.

FUN FACT

The Nashville Predators started in 1998. By 2018, the number of youth hockey players in Tennessee had doubled.

Superstar scorer Alex Ovechkin helped turn Washington, DC, into a hockey hotbed.

National Hockey League Map

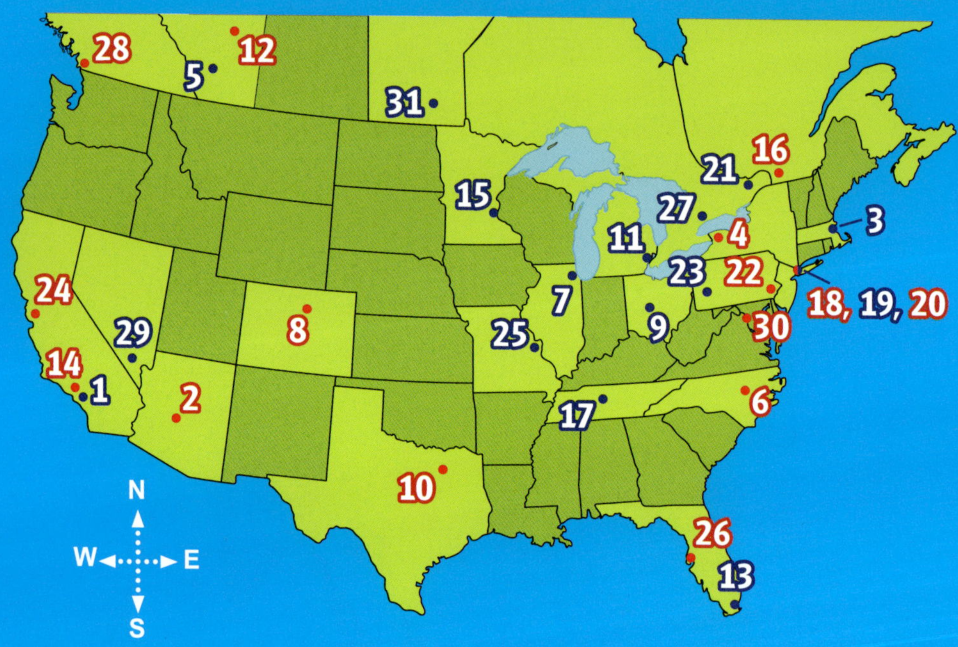

1. Anaheim Ducks
2. Arizona Coyotes
3. Boston Bruins
4. Buffalo Sabres
5. Calgary Flames
6. Carolina Hurricanes
7. Chicago Blackhawks
8. Colorado Avalanche
9. Columbus Blue Jackets
10. Dallas Stars
11. Detroit Red Wings
12. Edmonton Oilers
13. Florida Panthers
14. Los Angeles Kings
15. Minnesota Wild
16. Montreal Canadiens
17. Nashville Predators
18. New Jersey Devils
19. New York Islanders
20. New York Rangers
21. Ottawa Senators
22. Philadelphia Flyers
23. Pittsburgh Penguins
24. San Jose Sharks
25. St. Louis Blues
26. Tampa Bay Lightning
27. Toronto Maple Leafs
28. Vancouver Canucks
29. Vegas Golden Knights
30. Washington Capitals
31. Winnipeg Jets

The puck comes to Patrik Laine's stick. The Winnipeg Jets forward shoots it. Goal! The crowd cheers. But they're not in Winnipeg. They're not even in North America. The Jets are in Finland. That is Laine's home country.

The NHL is based in Canada and the United States. Playing games overseas helps grow the league. The first overseas game was in 1938. Teams played in England and France. In 2018, NHL teams played in four European countries. They also played in China.

Four teams in Canada played the first NHL season in 1917. Since that first season, the league has become well known across the globe.

The Jets' Patrik Laine greets fans before a practice in Helsinki, Finland.

BEYOND THE BOOK

After reading the book, it's time to think about what you learned. Try the following exercises to jumpstart your ideas.

THINK

DIFFERENT SOURCES. Think about what types of sources you could find about the NHL. What could you find in an encyclopedia? What could you learn on the internet? What about an interview with an NHL player? How could each of the sources be useful in its own way?

CREATE

PRIMARY SOURCES. A primary source is an original account of an event. Make a list of primary sources you might be able to find about the 1955 Stanley Cup Final. What new information might you learn from these sources?

SHARE

SUM IT UP. Write one paragraph summarizing the important points from this book. Make sure it's in your own words. Don't just copy what is in the text. Share the paragraph with a classmate. Does your classmate have any comments about the summary? Does he or she have additional questions about the NHL?

GROW

REAL-LIFE RESEARCH. What places could you visit to learn more about the Montreal Canadiens? What other things could you learn while you were there?

Visit www.ninjaresearcher.com/0738 to learn how to take your research skills and book report writing to the next level!

SEARCH LIKE A PRO
Learn about how to use search engines to find useful websites.

FACT OR FAKE?
Discover how you can tell a trusted website from an untrustworthy resource.

TEXT DETECTIVE
Explore how to zero in on the information you need most.

SHOW YOUR WORK
Research responsibly—learn how to cite sources.

WRITE

GET TO THE POINT
Learn how to express your main ideas.

PLAN OF ATTACK
Learn prewriting exercises and create an outline.

DOWNLOADABLE REPORT FORMS

Further Resources

BOOKS

Graves, Will. *Ultimate NHL Road Trip.* Abdo Publishing, 2019.

Kortemeier, Todd. *Superstars of the NHL.* Amicus, 2017.

Page, Sam. *Hockey: Then to WOW!* Liberty Street, 2017.

WEBSITES

FACTSURFER

Factsurfer.com gives you a safe, fun way to find more information.

1. Go to www.factsurfer.com.
2. Enter "National Hockey League" into the search box and click .
3. Select your book cover to see a list of related websites.

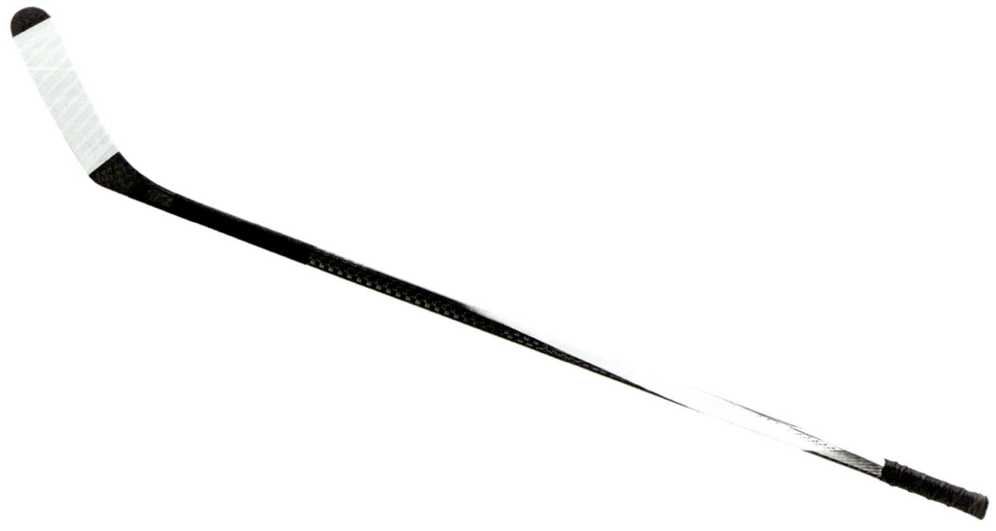

Glossary

check: In hockey, a check is when a player hits an opponent to stop him or her from getting to the puck. Auston Matthews checks his opponent to try to get the puck.

debuted: To have debuted is to have made one's first appearance. The Vegas Golden Knights debuted as the NHL's newest team in 2017.

dynasty: In sports, a dynasty is when a team wins multiple championships in a short amount of time. The Montreal Canadiens were a dynasty in the 1950s.

points: In hockey, players earn points for goals and assists. Wayne Gretzky led the NHL in points when he was nineteen years old.

rivalry: A rivalry is an ongoing and intense competition between two teams. The Detroit Red Wings and Chicago Blackhawks rivalry dates back to the Original Six era.

salary cap: A salary cap is a limit on how much teams can pay their players. Because of a strict salary cap, teams struggle to keep all of their good players together for long periods of time.

veteran: A veteran is a person who has a lot of experience in a certain field. Patrick Kane is a veteran on the Blackhawks.

Index

PHOTO CREDITS

The images in this book are reproduced through the courtesy of: Jeanine Leech/Icon Sportswire/AP Images, front cover (center); Adam Vilimek/Shutterstock Images, front cover (background); Kyle Besler/Shutterstock Images, p. 3; Nathan Denette/The Canadian Press/AP Images, pp. 4–5, 6–7, 9; Auspicious/Shutterstock Images, p. 8; ehrlif/Shutterstock Images, p. 10; AP Images, pp. 11, 12, 16–17, 20; Red Line Editorial, pp. 13 (chart), 26; Photo Works/Shutterstock Images, p. 13 (bottom); Pabkov/Shutterstock Images, p. 14; Ron Frehm/AP Images, pp. 18–19; Nam Y. Huh/AP Images, p. 21; David Duprey/AP Images, pp. 22–23; Jai Agnish/Shutterstock Images, p. 24; Ceri Breeze/Shutterstock Images, p. 25; Martti Kainulainen/Lehtikuva/AP Images, p. 27; Longchalerm Rungruang/Shutterstock Images, p. 30.

ABOUT THE AUTHOR

Kevin Frederickson is a freelance writer and editor from Ohio. He lives near Cincinnati with his golden doodle, Max.